번역 감수
준 한

미국 유학 중 숭산 큰스님의 가르침을 만나
2006년 덕숭총림 수덕사로 출가했다.
현재 서울 홍대선원과 소백산 양백정사 등에서
정진하고 있다.

부처님의 작은 선물

어른들을 위한 동시

부처님의 작은 선물

Buddha's Small Gifts

시·그림 **최승호**
번역 감수 **준 한**

담앤북스

시인의 말

마음은 부처님이 주신 선물이다.

그 마음으로 나는 시를 쓰고

그 마음으로 새들은 지저귀고

그 마음으로 꽃들은 피어난다.

마음, 그 값은 얼마인가.

세상에는 돈으로 계산할 수 없는 것들이 존재한다.

아이의 웃음은 얼마인가.

달빛과 고요는 얼마인가.

마음 기념관! 절은 부처님의 마음을 기억하고 기념하는 아름다운 공간이다. 그곳의 신비스런 사물들, 그곳에서의 스님들의 생활, 그리고 사찰을 둘러싼 대자연 속의 천진스러운 생명체들을 떠올리면서 시를 쓰고 그림을 그려 보았다.

선(禪)을 만나고 싶어 하는 외국인들을 위해 시의 번역 감수를 기꺼이 맡아 주신 홍대선원 준한 스님께 진심으로 감사드린다. 낮은 곳을 살피는 스님의 자비로운 마음으로 이 책이 한국인만의 것이 아닌, 그 누구의 것도 아닌 아름다운 선물의 색채를 띠게 되었다.

어느 해 봄날

최승호

CONTENTS

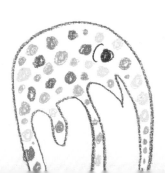

부처님의 ——— 작은 선물

청삽살개

도깨비가 왔나 봐
한밤중 청삽살개가 짖네
멍 멍 멍
꼬리를 흔들며 짖네

도깨비 반갑다고 짖나
숨바꼭질 하자고 짖나
멍 멍 멍

한밤중 청삽살개가 짖네
절마당 돌아다니며 짖네
멍 멍 멍

Blue Sapsal Dog[*]

I guess a goblin has come.
The blue sapsal dog is barking in the middle of the night.
Woof! Woof! Woof!
Wagging her tail and barking.

Is she barking to greet the goblin?
Is she barking to play hide and seek?
Woof! Woof! Woof!

The blue sapsal dog is barking in the middle of the night.
Barking around the temple yard.
Woof! Woof! Woof!

* Fluffy native dog that has been bred in Korea for a long time.

연꽃 도둑

연못
연꽃 한 송이
누가 훔쳐갔나

줄기의
이빨 자국 보니
고라니네

연꽃 도둑이
고라니라니

고라니도 부처님께
연꽃 한 송이 바치고 싶었나

Lotus Thief

In the Pond,
There was a lotus flower.
Who stole it?

On the stem,
I saw the teeth marks.
It's a river deer.

Who's the lotus thief?
The river deer?

Even the river deer wants.
Does she really want to offer a lotus flower to Buddha?

연등행렬

연등행렬이 숲속을 지나갑니다
너구리가 등을 들었어요
다람쥐도 등을 들었습니다
어두운 밤 숲이 환해졌어요

연못 물속으로 연등행렬이 지나갑니다
새우 눈이 환해졌어요
잉어 눈도 환해졌어요

연등행렬이 숲에서 마을로 내려갑니다
캄캄한 밤길 밝히며
연등들이 주렁주렁 마을로 내려갑니다

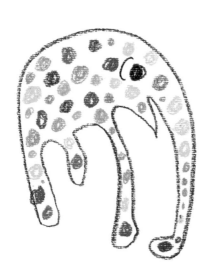

A Lotus Lantern Procession

A lotus lantern procession passes through the forest.
Raccoons are holding lanterns.
Squirrels also picked up lotus lanterns.
The dark night forest became bright.

The lotus lantern procession passes through the pond water.
Shrimp's eyes brightened up.
Carp's eyes also became brighter.

The lotus lantern procession goes down from the forest to the village.
Lighting up the dark night road,
Lotus lanterns are coming down to the village.

스님과 개구리

The Monk and Frog

마루 아래
섬돌
개구리 한 마리
비를 맞고 있네요
섬돌에서 마루로
뛰어오르고 싶은데
다리가 너무 작네요

어쩌나

마루에서 손이 하나 내려와
개구리를 마루 위로 올려주네요
스님의 손이네요
개구리와 스님이
마루에 나란히 앉아
비를 함께 바라보고 있네요

Under the Maru[*],
There is a seomdol[**].
There's a frog sitting there.
She's getting rained on.
From the Seomdol to the Maru,
She wants to jump.
But her legs are too small.

What should she do?

A hand comes down from the Maru.
To put the frog on the Maru.
It's a monk's hand.
The frog and monk.
Sitting side by side on the Maru,
They look at the rain together.

[*] Traditional Korean plank floor laid with gaps on the ground inside the house.

[**] Traditional Korean stone pavement placed at the front and back of a house for people to climb up and down.

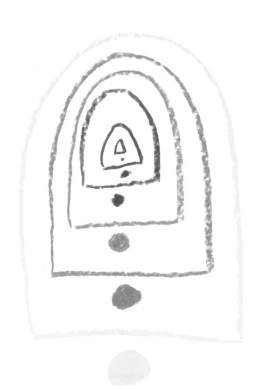

범종 소리

범종 소리에
황금색 햇빛이 번쩍번쩍

까마귀 눈부시겠다
베짱이도 눈부시겠어

범종 소리에
물비늘이 번쩍번쩍

잉어 눈부시겠다
새우도 눈부시겠어

The Sound of the Temple Bell

At the sound of the temple bell,
The golden sunlight sparkles.

The crows will be dazzled.
Even the grasshoppers would be dazzled.

At the sound of the temple bell,
The water scales sparkle.

The carp will be dazzled.
Even the shrimp would be dazzled.

돌미륵

큰 바위 아래
돌미륵이
우두커니 서 있네

비가 언제 그치려나

두꺼비가 엉금엉금 걸어와
돌미륵 곁에 앉아 있네

비가 언제 그치려나

Stone Maitreya

Under the big rock,
There is a stone Maitreya.
It stands there blankly.

When will the rain stop?

A toad crawls up.
It sits next to the stone mairteya.

When will the rain stop?

목어

스님이 목어에
색칠을 하네

스님
왜 벌거벗은 나무에 칠을 하세요

흠흠
이 나무물고기는 말이야
벌거벗고 있는 걸 싫어한단다
온몸에 아름다운 비늘을 두르듯이
옷 입는 걸 좋아하지

Wooden Carp

On the wooden carp,
A monk paints.

Hey, Monk.
Why paint bare wood?

Hmmm,
For this wooden fish,
It hates being naked.
Like having beautiful scales all over it's body,
It likes to wear clothes.

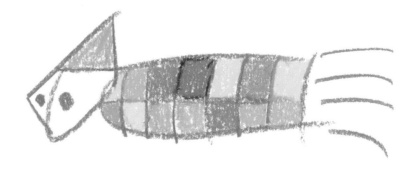

송사리들

스님이 물가에서
발을 씻고 있는데
송사리들이 몰려왔다

발의 때를 먹겠다고
송사리들이 덤벼든다

간지러워
그만 간질러
발바닥 그만 간지르라니까

The Minnows

At the water's edge,
A monk is washing his feet.
The minnows flocked in.

To eat the dirt on his feet,
The minnows rush in.

It tickles.
Stop it.
Stop tickling the soles of my feet.

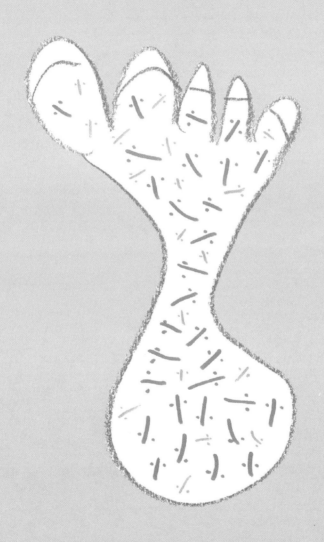

연잎 위에서

연잎 위에
넙죽
엎드려서
금개구리가 아침 해에 절을 합니다

해님
묵은 햇빛 안 주셔서 고맙습니다
날마다 싱싱한 햇빛만 주세요

28

On the Lotus Leaf

On the lotus leaf,
Flatly,
Lying down,
The golden frog bows to the morning sun.

Hey, Sun.
Thank you for not giving me the stale sunlight.
Just give me fresh sunlight every day.

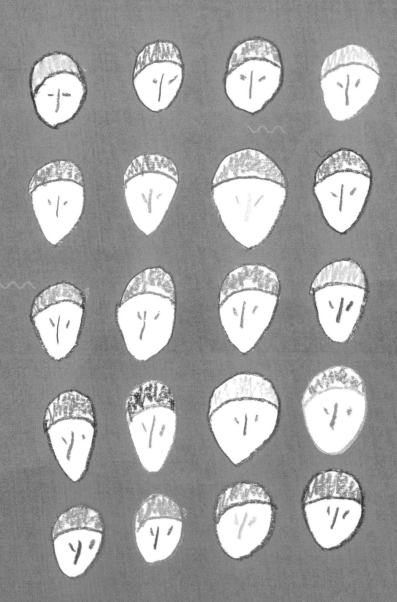

다람쥐들의 점심시간

오늘 점심은
도토리 한 알이다
누가 식판에
도토리 하나
놓고 간다

누구지?
다람쥐들이
고개를 들고 쳐다본다
스님이다

스님도 점심으로
도토리 한 알 먹나

Squirrels' Lunch Time

Today's lunch,
Is an acorn.
On the plate,
Someone puts an acorn.
And leaves.

Who is it?
Raising their heads,
Squirrels are watching.
He is a monk.

For lunch,
Monks also eat acorns?

The Goat Who Eats Paper Books

The book that contains Buddha's words,
The goat is munching on it.

No, you rascal.
He eats all by himself,
The Buddha's words.

Baa,
Baa-aaaaa.

종이책을 먹는 염소

부처님 말씀이 담긴 책을
염소가 우물우물 씹어먹는다

아니 이 놈이
부처님 말씀을
혼자 다 먹네

옴
옴매

털보깡충거미

털보깡충거미가
스님을 찾아왔어요

스님
저 거미줄 다 버리고 왔어요
제자로 받아주세요

어린 것이 수염이 제법 많구나
넌 우선 수염부터 깎아야겠다

Furry Jumping Spider

A furry jumping spider came,
To see a monk.

Hey, Monk.
I've left all those webs behind.
Please accept me as a disciple.

You have quite a bit of beard for a youngster.
You need to shave your beard first.

달밤

청삽살개 잠들었나
고요한 밤
달빛 환한 절 마당으로
박쥐 그림자 너울너울 날아다니네

고양이 잠들었나
고요한 밤
절 아래 흙벽돌집
박꽃 핀 지붕 위로
박쥐들 너울너울 날아다니네

The Moonlit Night

Does the blue sapsal dog fall asleep?
In the silent night,
To the moonlit temple yard,
The shadow of the bat is flying around.

Is the cat asleep?
In the silent night,
The mud brick house under the temple,
Above the roof where gourd flowers bloom,
Bats are waving around.

애벌레의 친구는 애벌레

그 애가 얼마 전까지만 해도
우리 애랑 잘 놀았는데
이제는 안 논답니다
그 애가 나비가 된 뒤로
우리 애랑은 안 논대요
놀아 주기는커녕
우리 애를 애, 애, 애벌레라고 놀린답니다
스님
어찌해야 하나요
우리 애가 친구 없다고 맨날 울어요

A Larva's Friend is a Larva

Until recently,
The kid had a good time with my child.
But now she won't play with him anymore.
Ever since the kid became a butterfly,
She doesn't play with my child.
She teases my child calling little, little, little larva.
Hey, Monk.
What should I do?
My child cries all the time because he has no friends.

부처꽃

부처꽃에
나비가 앉으면
눈이 향기롭지
입이 향기롭지
날개가 향기롭지

온몸이 향기로운 나비들이
너울너울
강 건너 마을로 날아가네
꼬
끼
오
낮닭 우는 마을로
향기를 나눠주러 날아가네

Buddha Flower

On the Buddha flower,
When a butterfly sits,
The eyes are fragrant,
The mouth is fragrant,
The Wings are fragrant.

Butterflies with fragrant bodies fly,
Waving around,
Across the river to the village.
Cock-a
-doodle
-doo.
To the village where roosters crow during the day,
Flying to share the scent.

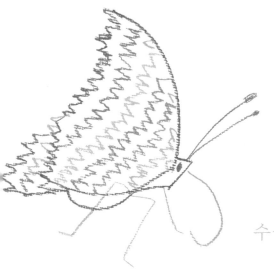

수풀떠들썩팔랑나비

수풀 수풀 떠들썩
떠들썩 떠들썩

수풀떠들썩팔랑나비 친구는
유리창떠들썩팔랑나비라네,

유리 유리 떠들썩
떠들썩 떠들썩

유리창떠들썩팔랑나비 친구는
수풀떠들썩팔랑나비라네

수풀 수풀 떠들썩
떠들썩 떠들썩

Bush-Bustler-Butterfly

Bushy, Bushy, Hustle and Bustle,
Fluttery, Fluttery.

The Bush-Bustler-Butterfly is my friend.
She is also the Window-Bustler-Butterfly.

Glass, Glass, Hustle and Bustle,
Fluttery, Fluttery.

The Window-Bustler-Butterfly is my friend.
She is also the Bush-Bustler-Butterfly.

Bushy, Bushy, Hustle and Bustle,
Fluttery, Fluttery.

솔부엉이

솔바람이 좋아
솔방울이 좋아
밤이면 솔잎 사이로 내려오는
달빛이 좋아
이슬이 좋아

나 솔밭에서 살래
솔부엉이로 살래

부엉
부엉

A Pine Owl

I like the pine breeze.
I like pine cones.
Coming down through the pine needles at night,
I like the moonlight.
I like the dew.

I want to live in a pine field.
I want to live as a pine owl.

hoot.
hoot.

푸르미르

미르 미르 푸르미르
푸른 용이지
푸른 하늘 나는 푸른 용이지

미리내 건너 가나
미리내 건너 오나

미르 미르 푸르미르
푸른 용이지
샛별 물고 날아오는
푸른 용이지

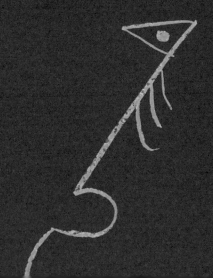

Purmir*

Mir, Mir, Purmir.
It's a blue dragon.
A blue dragon flying in the blue sky.

Is he going across Mirinae**?
Is he coming across Mirinae?

Mir, Mir, Purmir.
It's a blue dragon.
Flying with the morning star in his mouth,
It's a blue dragon.

* Korean native word meaning blue dragon.
** Korean native word for Milky Way.

겨울나기

굴뚝은 따뜻해

굴뚝에 뺨 대고
굴뚝새가 잠을 자고 있네요

Wintering

The chimney is warm.

With her cheek on the chimney,
The chimney bird is sleeping.

꼬마눈사람

그네를 타러
놀이터에 갔는데
꼬마눈사람이 그네에 앉아 있네

꼬마야 너
별꼬마거미 친구니
반달꼬마거미 친구니

꼬마눈사람은 말이 없네
아무 말이 없네
빙그레 웃기만 할 뿐

Little Snowman

To ride on a swing,
I went to the playground.
A little snowman is sitting on the swing.

Hey, Kid.
Are you a friend of the little star spider?
Are you a friend of the little half-moon spider?

The little snowman is speechless.
He doesn't say anything.
He just laughs and laughs.

소소리바람

소소리바람 불면
오소리는
굴속으로 들어가지

이제 긴 겨울이 올 거야
눈보라가 칠 거야

소소리바람 불면
너구리도 굴속으로 들어가지

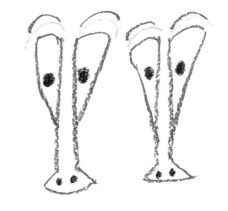

우리 굴 같이 쓸까
그래 그래

소소리바람 불면
오소리와 너구리는
굴속에서 바람 소리를 듣지

휘휘 휘휘
뭘 해야 하나
이 긴 겨울을 어떻게 견뎌야 하나

Sosoribaram*

When the Sosoribaram blows,
Into the cave,
The badgers disappear.

Now there will be a long winter.
There's going to be a snowstorm.

When the Sosoribaram blows,
Even raccoons go into the cave.

Shall we share the cave?
Yes, Yes.

When the Sosoribaram blows,
In the cave,
Badger and raccoon listen to the wind.

Whoosh, Whoosh.
What should we do?
How should we endure this long winter?

* Korean native word that refers to the cold,
  bitter wind that seems to seep into the flesh in early spring.

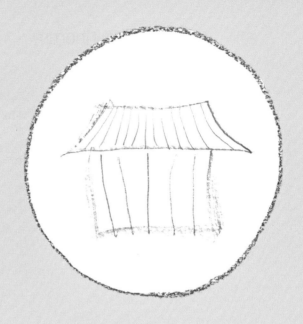

해우소

절에는 해우소가 있단다
해우소는
코뿔소와 달라
바다소와도 달라
하늘소와도 달라
해우소는 그 누구와도 싸우지 않아
그 누구에게도 화내지 않아
절에는 아주 평화로운
해우소가 있단다
어디에 있냐고?
스님한테 물어 보렴

Haewooso*

There is a Haewooso in the temple.
Haewooso is,
Different from a Kopulso**.
Different from a Badaso***.
Different from a Hanulso****.
Haewooso doesn't fight with anyone.
It doesn't get angry at anyone.
Very peaceful at the temple,
There is a Haewooso.
Where is it?
Just ask the monk.

* It has a dual meaning. It literally means a place to relieve your worries.
  It is used as the word for toilets in Korean.
** Rhinoceros.
*** Manatees.
**** Beetle.

하늘다람쥐

하늘하늘
하늘에서 내려오는
하늘다람쥐

도토리 먹으러 갈까
알밤 먹으러 갈까

하늘하늘
하늘에서
떡갈나무 숲으로 내려오는 하늘다람쥐

The Hanul-Squirrel[*]

Hanulhanul[**],
Coming down from the sky,
The Hanul-squirrel.

Let's go eat acorns.
Let's go eat chestnuts.

Hanulhanul,
From the sky,
Hanul-squirrel coming down to the oak forest.

[*]   Flying squirrel.
[**] Buoyantly.

도토리

도토리에서
떡잎들이 나왔네

나는 떡갈나무가 될 거야
나는 신갈나무가 될 거야
나는 상수리나무가 될 거야
아름드리 나무가 되어서
다람쥐들에게 도토리를 두루 나눠 줄 거야

그래 그래 우리 나중에
다람쥐들한테 도토리 많이 나눠주자

Acorns

From acorns,
The leaves have come out.

I will be an oak tree.
I will become a Mongolian oak.
I will become an old oak tree.
Becoming a large tree,
I'm going to hand out acorns to the squirrels.

Yeah, yeah, when that time comes,
Let's hand out a lot of acorns to the squirrels.

A Dazzlingly Beautiful Summer Day

On a beautiful summer day,
Clouds are flowing by.

On the ridge of beautiful summer day,
On the Zelkova trees of beautiful summer day,
On the hoopoes of beautiful summer day.

Butterflies are beautiful.
Flowers are beautiful.
Birds are beautiful.

On a dazzlingly beautiful summer day,
Mushy, Mushy,
Clouds are flowing by.

눈부시게 아름다운 여름날

아름다운 여름날
뭉게구름이 흘러가네

산등성이 아름다운 여름날
느티나무 아름다운 여름날
후투티 아름다운 여름날

나비가 아름답지
꽃이 아름답지
새가 아름답지

눈부시게 아름다운 여름날
뭉게뭉게
뭉게구름이 흘러가네

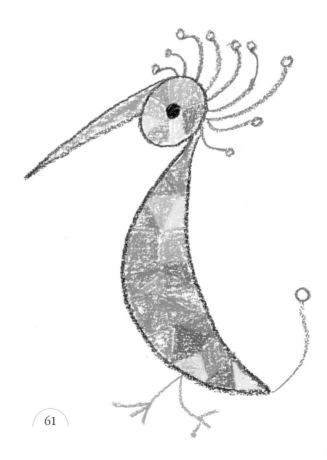

드렁칡 아래서 낮잠을

뻐드렁니를 드러낸 채
드르렁드르렁
심마니 할아버지가 코를 고네

드르렁드르렁
드르렁드르렁

다람쥐들이 귀를 막네
귀를 막을 게 아니라
심마니 할아버지 콧구멍을 막아야 하나

62

Take a Nap
under the Kudzu Tree

With buck teeth exposed,
Z-Z-Z,
Grandpa Simmani* snores.

z-z-z
Z-Z-Z

Squirrels are covering their ears.
Instead of covering our ears,
Should we plug Grandpa Simmani's nostrils?

* A Korean word meaning a person whose
 job is to dig up wild ginseng.

산 너머 산

휴
덥다
노새야
산 하나 넘으니까 또 산이 나타나지
우리 쉬다 갈까
넌 솔바람 쐬고 있어
난 물통에 시원한 샘물을 담아올게

The Mountain
Lying across the Mountain

Phew,
It's hot.
Hey, Mule.
After crossing one mountain, another mountain appears.
Should we take a rest?
You can enjoy the pine breeze.
I'll bring cool spring water in a bucket.

산길앞잡이를 따라서

나물 캐러 간 스님이
안개 자욱한 숲속에서
길을 잃었어요
이리 가도 안개
저리 가도 안개

스님 절 따라오세요

산길앞잡이를 따라서
스님이 산길을 내려옵니다
빈 바구니 들고
절 찾아 내려옵니다

고마워
안개 낀 날 또 보자

Following the
Mountain Road Guide

A monk went to gather wild herbs.
In the foggy forest,
He's lost.
Going this way, it's foggy.
Even if he goes another way, it's foggy.

Hey, Monk.
Please follow me.

Following the mountain road guide,
A monk comes down the mountain path.
Carrying an empty basket,
He comes down to find the temple.

Thank you.
See you again on a foggy day.

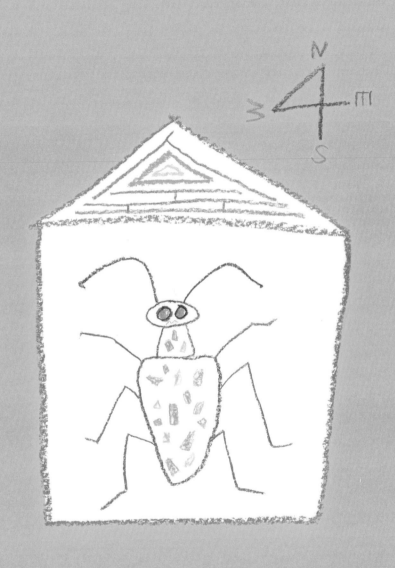

비빔밥

오늘은 새싹보리비빔밥을 먹을 거야

쓱싹쓱싹
고추장 넣고 비빌 거야

쓱싹쓱싹
참기름 넣고 비빌 거야

쓱싹쓱싹
고루고루 맛있게 비빌 거야

자 그럼 이제
아귀아귀 아귀처럼 먹어볼까

Bibimbap

Today I'm going to eat barley sprout bibimbap.

Mix, mix, mix.
I'm going to add gochujang paste and mix it together.

Mix, mix, mix.
I'm going to add sesame oil and mix it together.

Mix, mix, mix.
I will mix it thoroughly and deliciously.

Okay then now,
Munch, Munch.
Let's eat it like a monkfish.

황금색 허리띠를
두른 호박벌

황금색 허리띠를 두른 호박벌들이
호박공장 일꾼들처럼
호박꽃 속을 부지런히 들락거리네

긴 여름이 지나가네
가을이 오네

호박공장 문이 활짝 열린 것처럼
황금색 호박들이 여기저기
모습을 드러내네

고맙구나 고마워
할머니가 황금색 호박을 안고
호박벌들에게 인사하네
고맙구나 고마워

The Bumblebee
with a Golden Belt

Bumblebees wearing golden belts,
Like the pumpkin factory workers,
Diligently go in and out of the pumpkin blossoms.

The long summer passes by.
Autumn is coming.

As if the pumpkin factory door was wide open,
Here and there,
Golden pumpkins show itself.

Thank you. Thank you.
Grandma holding a golden pumpkin,
Says hello to the bumblebees.
Thank you. Thank you.

꿀

꿀벌 한 마리
잉잉대면서
스님을 쫓아가네

나 따라오지 마
나 꽃 아니야

그래도 꿀벌은 잉잉대면서
스님을 쫓아가지

내 몸에서 꿀 냄새가 나나
어제 꿀 한 숟갈 먹었는데
아직도 꿀 냄새가 나나

Honey

One honey bee,
Buzzing,
Chases the monk.

Don't follow me.
I'm not the flower.

Still, the honey bee is buzzing.
She chases after the monk.

Does my body smell like honey?
I ate a spoonful of honey yesterday.
Does it still smell like honey?

호롱불

나도밤나무도 캄캄하고
너도밤나무도 캄캄한 밤에
너도나도 불나방들이
호롱불에
모여드는 것은
불빛이 그리웠기 때문
어둠이 무서웠기 때문
숲속에서
혼자
외로웠기 때문

Kerosene Lamp

My chestnut forest is dark.
Even your chestnut forest is in the dark night.
You and I, fire moths gather,
Into the kerosene lamp.
Because we miss the light.
Because we are afraid of the dark.
In the forest,
Alone,
Because we are lonely.

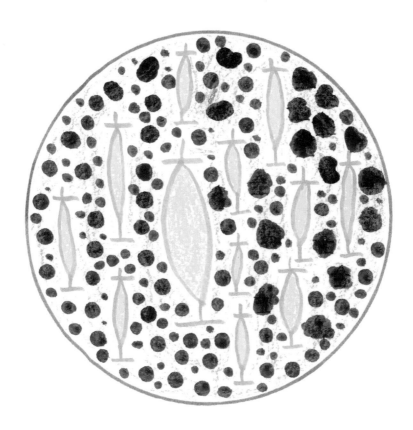

풍경 소리

댕그랑 댕그랑
봄바람이 왔어요
바다 건너 왔어요
산을 넘어 왔어요
댕그랑 댕그랑
이제 곧 제비꽃이 필 거예요
제비들이 날아다닐 거예요
댕그랑 댕그랑

Wind Chimes

Jingling, Jingling, Jingling.
The spring breeze has come.
It's come across the sea.
It's come over the mountain.
Jingle, Jingle, Jingle.
Violets will bloom soon.
Swallows will be flying around.
Jingle, Jingle, Jingle.

자라

심심해
연못가에 혼자 앉아 있으니까
심심해

자라야 심심하니
나도 심심해
나 심심한데
네 등에 나 좀 태워줄래

A Soft-Shelled Turtle

I'm bored.
Sitting alone by the pond,
I'm bored.

Are you bored, turtle?
I'm bored, too.
I'm bored so,
Can you give me a ride on your back?

빼꼼

판자울타리 구멍에
눈을 갖다 대고
밖을 내다보고 있는데
빼꼼
밖에서 누가
판자 구멍으로 나를 들여다본다

너 누구야
넌 누군데
나야 나
나가 누군데

Peephole

Through the hole in the fence,
Eyes to the hole,
I'm looking out.
Peek.
Someone outside,
Looking at me through the hole in the fence.

Who are you? I'm asking.
Who are you? he asks.
It's me,
Me is who?

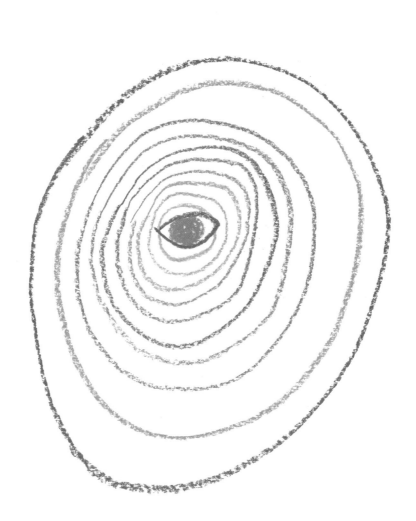

땅강아지

땅따먹기 하던 아이들이
집으로 다 돌아간 저녁에
어둑어둑
땅거미가 지네요

땅을 파고 흙을 파며
아직도 누가 어스름 속에
혼자 놀고 있네요

땅강아지야
너 집에 안 가니

A Mole Cricket

Children were playing Ttangttameokgi*.
In the evening when everyone returned home,
It was getting dark.
Dusk was falling.

Digging the ground and digging the soil,
Who is still in the twilight?
I'm playing alone.

Hey, Mole Cricket.
Aren't you going home?

* One of Korea's traditional children's games.
  Each person draws a line on the designated land by striking a tiny stone with
  his or her finger, and then the land is taken away.

다락방 다람쥐

휘휘
밤바람 분다

잠 못 드는 다람쥐
다락방 다람쥐

범 내려오면 어쩌나
삵 내려오면 어쩌나

잠 못 드는 다람쥐
다락방 다람쥐

콩알만 한 심장이
콩닥콩닥

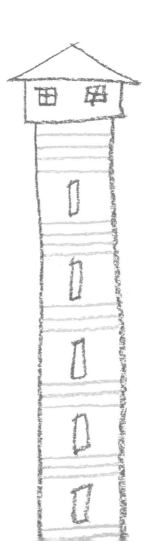

The Attic Squirrel

Woo-oo-oo,
The night wind blows.

Squirrel can't sleep well.
The attic squirrel.

What if the tiger comes down?
What if the cat comes down?

Who is the sleepless squirrel?
The attic squirrel.

Her pea-size heart is pounding.
Pit-a-pat. Pit-a-pat.

비 오는 날의
비오리

비 오는 날 비오리는
비를 그냥 맞지요
비에 그냥 젖지요
우산 같은 건 안 씁니다

비 오는 날 비오리는
머리에 비를 이고 가는 것처럼
목을 바로 세우고 여울을 건너갑니다

오리발을 저으며
물살을 가르며
찰랑찰랑 여울을 거뜬하게 건너갑니다

The Water Pheasant
on a Rainy Day

There is a water pheasant on a rainy day.
Just getting rained on,
Just getting wet in the rain,
She doesn't use umbrellas or anything like that.

There is a water pheasant on a rainy day.
Like carrying rain on her head,
She straightens her neck and crosses the rapids.

Waving webfeet,
Cutting through the current of water,
She crosses the rapids with ease.

병아리와의 이별

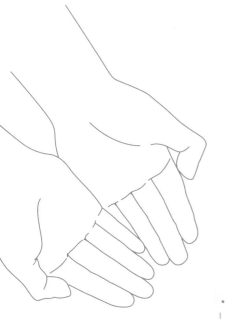

병아리 상자
머리에 이고
할머니가 장터로 가네

팔려 가는 것도 모르고
병아리들은
할머니 머리 위에서 삐약 삐약

멀리서 암탉은
꼬꼬댁 꼭꼭
병아리들을 부르고 있네

Farewell to the Chick

With a box of chicks,
On her head,
Grandma is going to the local marketplace.

Unaware that they are being sold,
On her head,
The chicks cheep-cheep.

A hen from afar,
Cluck, Cluck, Cluck,
She's calling the chicks.

내 호주머니 속의 주머니쥐

내 호주머니 속의 주머니쥐가
숨 막히면 어쩌나
호주머니에 구멍을 뻥
뚫어야 하나

뻥 뚫린 구멍으로
주머니쥐가 달아나면 어쩌나
호주머니 안에 맛있는 호두를
넣어두어야 하나

The Possum in My Pocket

A possum in my pocket.
What if she suffocates?
Going pop in my pocket,
Should I punch a hole?

Through a gaping hole,
What if the possum runs away?
Maybe, she likes delicious walnuts.
Should I keep it in my pocket?

누룽지를 먹는 개

누룽 누룽 누룽지
누가 먹나요
햇볕에 바짝 말린 누룽지
멍석에 바짝 말린 누룽지

이 누룽지 맛있겠다
이웃집 개 바둑이가
누룽지 깨작깨작 씹어보다가
맛이 별로라고

긴 혀 늘어뜨리고
제 집으로 털레털레 돌아갑니다

The Dog Who Eats Nurungji [*]

Nurung Nurung Nurungji.
Who eats it?
Nurungji dried in the sun.
Nurungji dried on a mat.

This nurungji looks delicious.
A piece of the nurungji,
My neighbor's dog Baduk chewed on.
She didn't think it tastes good.

Long tongue hanging out,
She runs back to her house.

[*] Rice scorched and stuck to the bottom of a pot,
a traditional Korean snack.

지우개

무지개를 지우는
지우개가
있었다

무지개를 지우고
지우다 보면
자기 몸이 무지개로 얼룩진
지우개가 있었다

Eraser

There was an eraser.
That could erase,
The rainbow.

Erasing the rainbow,
Erasing and erasing it,
It's body is stained with a rainbow.
There was such an eraser.

조랑말

조롱 조롱 조롱박이 열리는
조롱박덩굴 아래로
조그만 수레 끌며
조랑말이 저녁에 왔네
딸랑딸랑
수레에 조롱박들 실으러 왔네

호롱불을 켜야겠어

어둑어둑 초저녁 길
호롱불 목에 걸고
조랑말이 수레 끌며 마을로 가네
집집마다 등불 밝힌 마을로 가네

A Pony

Cala cala calabash hanging down,
Under the calabash vines,
Pulling a small cart,
The pony came in the evening.
Jingling, Jingling,
She came to load the cart with calabashes.

We should turn on the lantern.

On the road in the early evening,
With a lantern around her neck,
A pony goes to town pulling a cart.
To a village where every house is lit with lanterns.

악어의 생일

무지개떡 먹으면서 다짐한다
무지개처럼 고운 마음씨로 살자
남을 물어뜯지 말자
다시는 싸우지 말자

Crocodile's Birthday

I make a promise while eating rainbow rice cake.
Let's live with a heart as kind as a rainbow.
Don't bite others.
Let's never fight again.

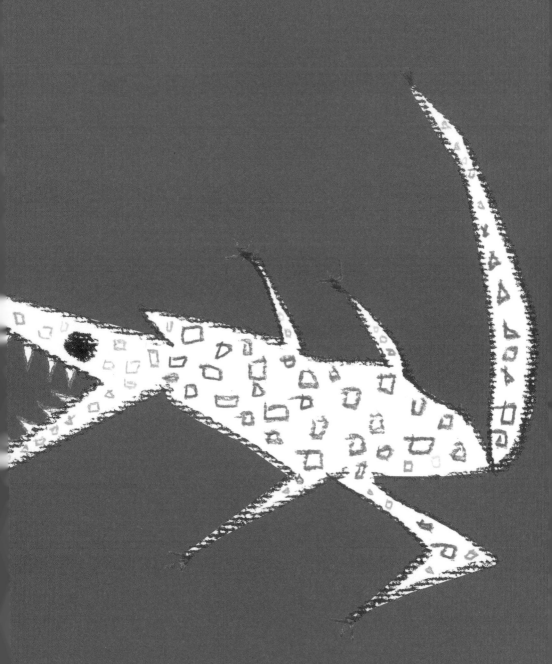

소쩍새

아무도 없나요
나 혼자 어둠 속에 있나요
왜 아무도 대답이 없나요
소쩍
소쩍

A Little Owl

Is there anyone here?
Am I alone in the dark?
Why is no one answering?
Hoot.
Hoot.

우산버섯

베짱이야
비 맞지 말고 이리 와
우리가 우산 씌워줄게
어서 오라니까
비 맞으면 춥잖아
어! 그냥 가네
왜 비를 혼자 맞으면서 가지
우리가 모르는 무슨 슬픈 일이
베짱이에게 있었나

The Umbrella Mushroom

Hey, Grasshopper.
Come here, don't get caught in the rain.
We'll put you under an umbrella.
I told you to come here.
It's cold when it rains.
Uh! she just goes.
Why are you going out in the rain alone?
Something sad we don't know,
Did the grasshopper go through?

봄

겨울산 속에 엎드려 있던
캄캄한 개구리들
눈이 열렸습니다
입이 열렸습니다
귀가 열렸습니다
개구리들이 산을 내려갑니다

어서 오시오
눈 열린 개구리들

먼저 입 열린 개구리들이
개굴 개굴
개굴 개굴
논에서 노래합니다
연못에서 늪에서 반갑다고 노래합니다
개굴 개굴
개굴 개굴

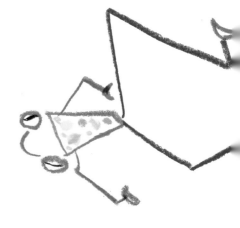

Spring

Lying face down in the winter mountains,
There are frogs in the dark.
Eyes are opened.
Mouths are opened.
Ears are opened.
Frogs go down the mountain.

Welcome,
Frogs with open eyes.

The frogs who opened their Mouths earlier sing.
Croak. Croak.
Croak. Croak.
Singing in the rice fields,
From the pond to the swamp,
they sing to welcome each other.
Croak. Croak.
Croak. Croak.

띄엄띄엄 아름다운 징검다리

피라미 비늘 반짝이는 해질녘이다
물비늘 반짝이는 해질녘이다

띄엄띄엄 징검다리
개여울 징검다리

거위들이 집으로 돌아가는 해질녘이다
오리들이 집으로 돌아가는 해질녘이다

거위는 뒤뚱뒤뚱
오리는 꽥꽥

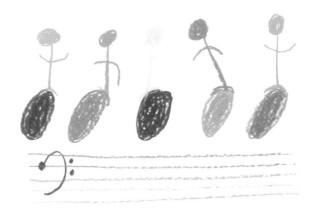

The Babbling
Beautiful Stepping Stones

It's a sunset where the minnow's scales sparkle.
It's a sunset with sparkling water scales.

Sporadic stepping stones.
Gaeyeoul* stepping stones.

It's a sunset when the geese return home.
It's a sunset when the ducks return home.

The goose waddles.
Ducks quack.

* Korean word meaning a place where the bottom of a river is
  shallow or narrow and the current flows strongly.

돼지감자 뚱딴지

돼지 먹는 돼지감자
먹어도 되나
먹어도 되지

돼지감자 뚱딴지
안 먹어도 되나
안 먹어도 되지

화분에 심어도 되나
심어도 되지

심으면 꽃 피나
꽃 핀다

The Pig Potato, Ttungddanji*

Pig eating pig potato.
Can I eat it?
I can eat it.

Pig Potato Ttungddanji.
Can I not eat it?
I don't have to eat it.

Can I plant it in a flower pot?
I can plant it.

If I plant it, will it bloom?
Flowers would bloom.

* Korean word that refers to a person whose behavior or
  way of thinking is awkward.

돌하르방

참새는 참
하필이면
돌하르방 머리에 똥을 싸냐
그래도 돌하르방은 웃네
괜찮다
괜찮아
괜찮다니까
돌하르방은 웃네

Dolhareubang[*]

Hey, sparrow you scamp!
Of all occasions.
Why do you poop on Dolhareubang's head?
But Dolhareubang is smiling.
Okay,
You are okay.
Sure, it's okay.
Dolhareubang is smiling.

* The guardian stone god, meaning grandfather made of stone,
  is believed to protect and bring safety and order to Jeju Island in Korea.

드렁허리

드렁 드렁 드렁허리
드렁허리 아시나요

두렁 두렁 논두렁에
드렁허리 살지요
논두렁에 숨어서
혼자 살지요

드렁 드렁 드렁허리
배고픈 밤이면
논에 나와 개구리 잡아먹나요
개구리 먹고 드렁드렁
논두렁에 숨어 혼자 자나요

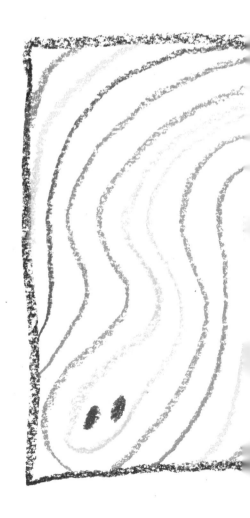

Albino Swamp Eel

Albino, albino, albino eel.
Do you know albino swamp eel?

Swamp, swamp, on the rice field swamp,
Albino swamp eel lives comfortably.
Hiding in the rice field swamp,
She lives alone.

Swamp, swamp, swamp eel.
On hungry nights,
Does she come out to the rice fields and eat frogs?
Eating a frog and crying,
Does she hide in the rice field and sleep alone?

심퉁이

이놈 별명은
심퉁이랍니다
심통 사납게 생겨서
심퉁이지요
오늘도 심퉁이가
심통이 잔뜩 났네요
심퉁아
얼굴 구겨졌다
얼굴 펴라
얼굴 확 펴라니까

Simtungi[*]

The nickname of this guy.
Is Simtungi.
Because he looks like a bad tempered fierce.
He's called Simtungi.
How is she feeling today?
He has a lot of bad temper.
Hey, Simtungi.
Your face crumpled.
Straighten your face.
I told you to straighten your face.

[*] Korean word meaning a person with an unkind heart and a lot of greed, or a smooth lumpfish.

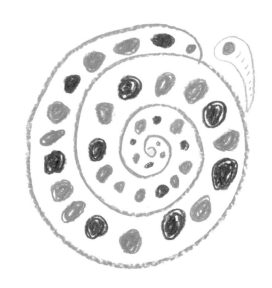

돌탑

돌탑을 쌓자
돌탑을 쌓자

여울물 속 물여우는
달 뜨는 밤이면 돌탑을 쌓지
물여우나비가 되게 해주세요
소원을 빌면서 돌탑을 쌓지

달님에게 빌면서
돌탑을 쌓지
소원을 빌면서 돌탑을 쌓지

Stone Tower

Let's build a stone tower.
Let's build a stone tower.

The water fox in the rapid water.
When the moonlit night comes, she builds a stone tower.
Please make her a water fox butterfly.
She builds a stone tower while making a wish.

Praying to the moon,
While making a wish,
She builds a stone tower.

댕댕이바구니 속의 댕댕이

우리 귀염둥이 댕댕이가
댕댕이바구니 속에서 잠을 자네요

꿈속에서 고양이랑 다투는 건지
이따금 코를 찡그리고
이빨을 살짝 드러내면서
우리 재롱둥이 댕댕이가
댕댕이바구니 속에서 잠을 자네요

귀염둥이 우리 댕댕이
재롱둥이 우리 댕댕이

The Dog
in the Doggy Basket

Our cutie doggy,
The dog is sleeping in a doggy basket.

Is she fighting with a cat in her dream?
Wrinkling her nose sometimes,
Showing her teeth barely,
Our playful dog is sleeping in the doggy basket.

Our cutie doggy.
Our playful doggy.

달과 원숭이

긴팔원숭이들이
장대 들고
달 따러 가는 밤에

긴코원숭이들이
국자를 들고
물속의 달을 건지고 있네

달님이 웃네
원숭이들이 나를 웃기는구나
물속의 달을 국자로 건지다니

The Moon and Monkey

The monkey has pretty very long arms.
Holding a pole,
On a night when she goes to look for the moon.

The monkey has such a long nose.
Holding a ladle,
She's lifting the moon from the water.

The moon is smiling.
Monkeys make me laugh.
How can you ladle the moon in the water?!

호랑이콩

땅을 찢고
떡잎을 내밀었네

아기 호랑이가
두 귀를 내민 것처럼

Tiger Bean*

Tearing up the ground,
She puts out a cotyledon.

Like a baby tiger.
Sticking out both ears.

* In Korea, cranberry beans are called
tiger beans because they have a tiger pattern.

하늘지기

등대지기 할아버지
등대를 지킬 때

하늘지기는
논두렁에 앉아서
하늘을 지키나요

우리 눈엔 하늘도둑 안 보이는데
하늘지기 눈에는 하늘 훔쳐가는
하늘도둑도 보이나요

The Sky Keeper

Lighthouse keeper grandpa.
When guarding the lighthouse.

The sky keeper.
Sitting on the rice field ridge,
Does he protect the sky?

The sky thief is invisible to our eyes.
In the eyes of the sky keeper,
Can he see the sky thief who is stealing the sky?

용궁

쥐가오리가 가오리까
노랑가오리가 가오리까
아니면 전기가오리가 가오리까

흠
우리 용왕님께서는
전기가오리 먼저 들라 하신다
등불을 환히 밝히고
아름다운 용궁을 지어보자

The Palace of Sea King

Will manta rays visit there at lightning speed?
Will sting rays visit there at lightning speed?
Or will electric rays visit there at lightning speed?

Hmm,
Her Majesty,
She commands that the electric rays come in first.
Lighting up the lamp brightly,
Let's build a beautiful sea palace.

칠성장어가
칠성무당벌레에게

나는 가끔
내가 북두칠성에서 왔다는 생각이 들어
그리고 언젠가는 내가 다시
북두칠성으로 돌아간다는 생각이
들고는 하지

칠성무당벌레야
너도 그런 생각 들지 않니

From the Seven Star Eel*
to the Seven Star Ladybird *

I think sometimes.
I feel like I'm from the Big Dipper.
And someday I'll come back.
The idea of returning to the Big Dipper.
I can't stop thinking.

Hey, Seven star ladybird.
Don't you feel the same way?

In Korea, lamprey eels are called seven-star eels because they
have seven gill slits.

In Korea, seven-spot ladybirds are called seven-star ladybugs
because of the seven spots on their backs.

부처님의 작은 선물

부처님이 마음을 선물하셨네
마음은
얼마나 작은지
민들레 씨 속으로 들어가지
환한 꽃을 피우지

부처님이 마음을 선물하셨네
마음은
얼마나 작은지
노랑나비 눈 속으로 들어가지
날개를 치게 하지
너울너울 밝은 하늘을 날게 하지

Buddha's Small Gift

Buddha gave his heart as a gift.
How small,
His heart is!
It can get inside a dandelion seed.
It blooms brightly.

Buddha gave his heart as a gift.
How small,
His heart is!
It can go inside the eyes of a yellow butterfly.
It makes her flap her wings.
Fluttery. Fluttery.
It makes her fly in the bright sky.

부처님의 작은 선물

초판 1쇄 발행 2024년 5월 15일

시 · 그림 최승호
번역 감수 준한

펴낸이 오세룡
편집 허승 여수령 정연주 손미숙 박성화 윤예지
기획 곽은영 최윤정
디자인 고혜정 김효선 최지혜
홍보·마케팅 정성진

펴낸곳 담앤북스
주소 서울특별시 종로구 새문안로3길 23 경희궁의 아침 4단지 805호
대표전화 02-765-1250(편집부) 02-765-1251(영업부)
전송 02-764-1251
전자우편 dhamenbooks@naver.com

출판등록 제300-2011-115호

ISBN 979-11-6201-429-5 03810

정가 16,800원